How the
Camel
got his Hump

Retold by Robert James

Illustrated by Stefania Colnaghi

Crabtree Publishing Company

www.crabtreebooks.com

Crabtree Publishing Company
www.crabtreebooks.com
1-800-387-7650

PMB 59051, 350 Fifth Ave.
59th Floor,
New York, NY 10118

616 Welland Ave.
St. Catharines, ON
L2M 5V6

Published by Crabtree Publishing in 2012
Printed in the U.S.A./052012/FA20120413

Series editor: Jackie Hamley
Editor: Kathy Middleton
Proofreader: Reagan Miller
Series advisor: Catherine Glavina
Series designer: Peter Scoulding
Production coordinator and
   Prepress technician: Margaret Amy Salter
Print coordinator: Katherine Berti

Text © Franklin Watts 2010
Illustration © Stefania Colnaghi 2010

The rights of Robert James to
be identified as the author
and Stefania Colnaghi as the
illustrator of this Work have
been asserted.

First published in 2010
by Franklin Watts
(A division of Hachette
Children's Books)

Library and Archives Canada
Cataloguing in Publication

CIP available at Library and Archives Canada

Library of Congress
Cataloging-in-Publication Data

CIP available at Library of Congress

This story tries to explain
some of the different things
we see in the world today.
It was originally written by
an author called Rudyard
Kipling, over 100 years ago.

Long ago, when the world was new, there was much work to do.

3

The animals worked
hard, but Camel
was lazy.

The desert god
saw this.

"Why are you so lazy, Camel?" he asked.

"Humph!"
said Camel.

9

"You are very rude,"
said the desert god.

"Humph!" said Camel.

Furious, the desert god
cast a spell.

Camel's back puffed up.

"Now you will work!"
said the desert god.

"How can I work with this on my back?" cried Camel.

17

"With that on your back, you can work for days without eating or drinking!" said the desert god.

And that is how Camel got his humph—or hump, as we call it today.

21

Puzzle Time!

Put these pictures in the right order and tell the story!

rude

annoyed

lazy

angry

Which words describe Camel and
which describe the desert god?

Turn the page for the answers!

Notes for adults

TADPOLES: TALES are structured for emergent readers. The books may also be used for read-alouds or shared reading with young children.

How the Camel got his Hump is based on a classic story by Rudyard Kipling. This kind of story is known as a "just-so" or "porquoi" story because it explains how something came to be. For example, many of Kipling's stories explain how certain animals developed their unique characteristics. Since young children are often curious and filled with questions, "just-so" stories make ideal reading material.

IF YOU ARE READING THIS BOOK WITH A CHILD, HERE ARE A FEW SUGGESTIONS:

1. Make reading fun! Choose a time to read when you and the child are relaxed and have time to share the story.

2. Explain that the story is called a "just so" or "pourquoi" story. *Porquoi* is a French word that means "why." Pourquoi stories are tales that explain why or how something is in the world. This information will help set a purpose for reading.

3. Encourage the child to reread the story and to retell it using his or her own words. Invite the child to use the illustrations as a guide.

4. Encourage the child to use his or her imagination to think of other "just-so" story topics. What "why" or "how" questions about animals can they think of?

5. Give praise! Children learn best in a positive environment.

HERE ARE OTHER TITLES FROM TADPOLES: TALES FOR YOU TO ENJOY:

VISIT WWW.CRABTREEBOOKS.COM FOR OTHER CRABTREE BOOKS.

Answers
Here is the correct order:
1. d 2. e 3. a 4. b 5. f 6. c

Words to describe Camel:
lazy, rude

Words to describe the desert god:
annoyed, angry